FARLEY GOES TO THE DOCTOR

By Emily Perl Kingsley
Illustrated by Maggie Swanson

A SESAME STREET/READER'S DIGEST KIDS BOOK

Published by Reader's Digest Young Families, Inc.,
in cooperation with Children's Television Workshop

"Today's the day we see Dr. Rothman for your checkup," Farley's daddy said.

"But, Daddy," said Farley, "I'm not sick. Why do I have to go to the doctor?"

Farley's daddy explained. "You need a checkup every year so the doctor can make sure you are well and can see how much you've grown."

"Will the doctor give me a shot?" asked Farley.
"I don't like shots."

"Maybe," said his daddy. "I'm not sure. Dr. Rothman will tell us if you need one."

"I think I will take T. J. Bear," said Farley. "Just to keep me company."

When Farley and his daddy arrived at the doctor's office, they met Ernie coming out the door.

"Hi, Ernie," said Farley. "What are you doing here?"

"I have a sore throat," whispered Ernie. "Dr. Rothman gave me some medicine to make it better."

Inside the doctor's waiting room, Farley hung
up his jacket and played with a train set while he
waited for his turn.

After a while the nurse, Mrs. Williams, came
into the waiting room. "You may come in now,
Farley," she said, "and bring your daddy."

In the examining room Daddy helped Farley
take off his clothes.

"Now," said the nurse, "let's see how tall you
are and how much you weigh."

Farley stood up on the scale, and Nurse Williams measured him with the height bar.

"You've grown a lot in the last year," she said. "You're forty-two inches tall." Mrs. Williams wrote Farley's height on his chart.

"May I measure my bear?" Farley asked.

"Let's measure him with this ruler," said the nurse. "Hmm. He seems to be just the right height for a bear."

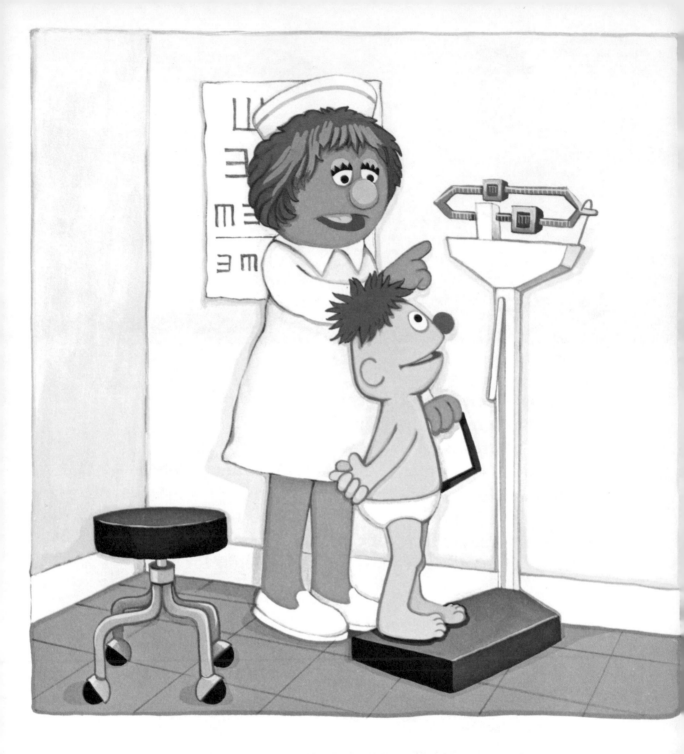

"Now," said Mrs. Williams, "let's see how much you weigh." She moved the weights across the top of the scale. "Thirty-eight pounds," she said. "That's a good weight for a boy your height."

"May we weigh T.J.?" asked Farley.

"Yes," said Mrs. Williams. "Let's weigh him on the baby scale."

Just then Dr. Rothman came in. "Hi, Farley," she said. "I see that you brought along a friend."

"Hi, Doctor. My teddy needs a checkup, too," said Farley.

"Sit down on that table and let me look at your throat, Farley," said Dr. Rothman.

Farley climbed onto the table. "Open wide, please," said Dr. Rothman. She placed a tongue depressor in Farley's mouth. "Now say AHHHHHHHH," she said.

"AHHHHHHHH," said Farley. Dr. Rothman shined a little flashlight in his mouth.

"Your throat looks fine, Farley," said Dr. Rothman. "It doesn't look sore like Ernie's."

"May I see if my teddy bear has a sore throat?" asked Farley.

"Don't forget to tell him to say AHHHHHHHH," said Daddy.

"T.J. always says GRRRR," said Farley.

Dr. Rothman shined the little flashlight
into Farley's ears. "Your ears look healthy, too,"
she said. "Would you like to use my flashlight
to check your teddy's ears?"

"Oh, thanks," said Farley.

Farley looked at T.J.'s ears with the doctor's flashlight.

"They are very furry," said Farley.

"That's right," said Dr. Rothman. "Normal ears for a bear."

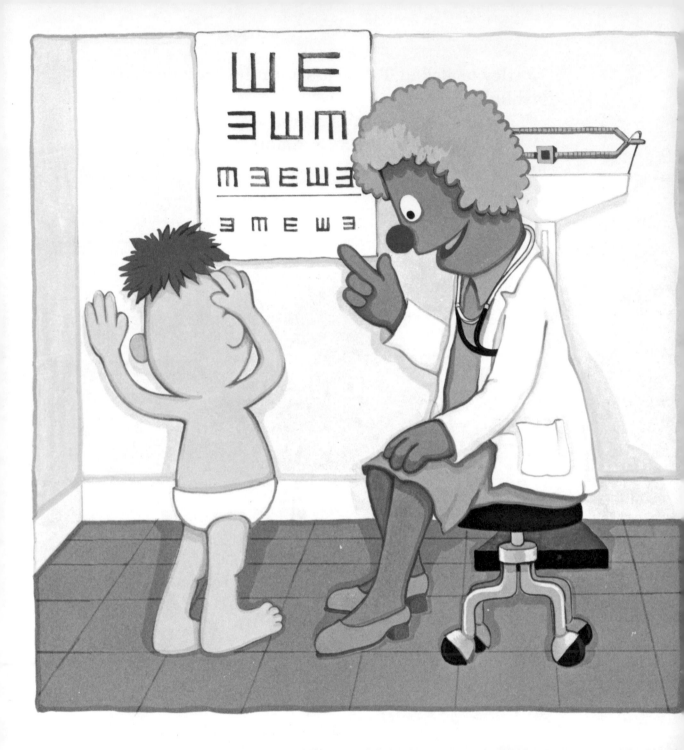

"Hop down, Farley. I want to check your eyes," said Dr. Rothman.

She pointed to the *E*'s on the eye chart. "Show me which way the *E*'s are pointing," she said.

"It's your turn, T.J.," said Farley.
"Your teddy has good eyesight, too," said the doctor.

"This is a stethoscope," said Dr. Rothman. "It's going to feel cold when I hold it to your chest." She placed the stethoscope on Farley's chest. After a minute she said, "I can hear your heart beating. Would *you* like to hear your heart, Farley?"

"Oh, yes," said Farley. "Wow! It sounds just like a drum. Thump-thump, thump-thump, thump-thump."

"That's right," said the doctor. "Your heart sounds good and strong."

"This is called a stethoscope, T.J.," said
Farley. "It's going to feel cold. Now hold still so
I can listen to your heart."

Dr. Rothman felt Farley's neck, his tummy, and under his arms.

"That tickles!" Farley giggled.

"I'm almost through," said the doctor. "You seem to be in tip-top shape."

"Does that tickle, T.J.?" Farley asked as he poked his teddy bear in the tummy.

"Now I'm going to tap your knees with this
little rubber hammer," said Dr. Rothman. "Ready?"
The doctor tapped one of Farley's knees. His
leg gave a little jerk. Then she tapped the
other knee, and that leg jerked, too.
"That's just what your legs are supposed to
do," said Dr. Rothman. "Your reflexes are good."

Dr. Rothman asked Farley to walk across the room so she could see if his back was straight.

"I'm writing on your chart that you have very good posture," said the doctor.

"T.J. does, too," said Farley. "See how straight his back is?"

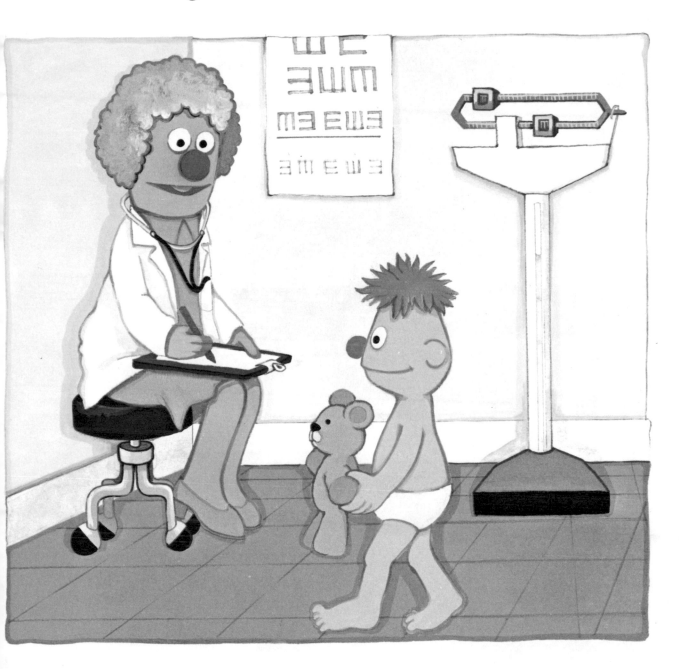

"Well," said Dr. Rothman. "There's only one thing left to do. Your chart shows that it's time for you to have a measles shot."

"Will it hurt?" asked Farley.

"The shot will only hurt for a minute," said the doctor, "but it will keep you from getting the measles."

The doctor gave Farley the measles shot in his arm.

"Ouch!" said Farley.

"That's all," said Dr. Rothman.

"You're lucky, T.J.," said Farley. "Teddy bears don't have to get shots."

"Well, Farley," said Dr. Rothman, "I'm happy to say that you're very healthy. Take this card home and show it to your mommy. It tells your height and weight and says that you got your measles shot. You'll need to give the card to your school nurse when you start school."

"Good-bye, Dr. Rothman," said Farley.

"Thank you," said Farley's daddy.

"Hurry up, Dad," said Farley as they walked home. "I want to give my elephant and my giraffe and *all* of my stuffed animals a checkup!"